UP Keeps the Light ON!

Book 2 of the UP Series

Written and Illustrated by the Children
of Hope Town Primary School,
Elbow Cay, Abaco, Bahamas
2014 - 2015

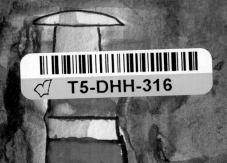

If you have ever wondered about the workings
of our lighthouse, this book will guide the way.

The Bahamian Lighthouses were built to keep ships safely in deep water and away from the shoals of the shallow Bahama Banks. Each lighttower had its own *Daymark*, a distinctly different paint scheme, either solid or striped, that was visible during daylight hours. After dark, each lighthouse flashed a unique *Flash Pattern* with the light of its Fresnel lens. Mariners were able to establish their location when seeing a lighthouse by referring to pilot books and paper charts. Even today, this more primitive method of navigation is in use as a backup to GPS.

For nearly 100 years, the flash pattern "GP FL W 5 EV 15 Sec 120FT 15M" of our lighthouse has warned mariners away from the dangerous Elbow Reef, thereby allowing them safe passage. The light is defined on the chart as a white light, which flashes 5 times every 15 seconds, is 120 ft. above sea level and is seen at a distance of 15-20 miles.

This book is dedicated to its creators—the students of Hope Town Primary School.

Copyright © 2015 Heather Forde-Prosa
Sulick Studio Press

ISBN: 978-0-99100990902

Library of Congress Control Number 2015934233

Printed June, 2015, in the United States of America by Southeastern Printing, Stuart, FL.

*UP teaches all of us to aim high, try new things, persevere
and never underestimate the power of friendship.*

This book came together with the support and assistance of friends:
Annie Potts, Attila Feszt, Deanne Albury, Aimee Lederhause, Justin Higgs, Donnella Rolle,
Bill County, Susan Roberts, Susan Sandberg, Erika Feszt-Russell, Mary Balzac, Tom Gearen,
Lorraine Sulick-Morecraft, Bonnie Rupe, Beth Maschinot, Susan Abbott, Lisa Ballard,
Teleri Jones, Trudy Eagan and Stephanie Sweeting.

As UP would say, *"It's great to have friends"* I thank you all so very much for your help.
~Heather Forde-Prosa

In a tiny Lizard Lodge in the little village of Hope Town lives a young lizard named UP.

He lives up to his name every day because he always wakes up before everyone else in the house, even before the sunrise!

It is Regatta time in Abaco and UP is on the dock watching the sailboats enter Hope Town Harbour for the night. He notices that the lighthouse keeper, Mr. Elvis Jeffery, does not look happy.

Wondering why he looks sad, UP asks, "What is the matter?"

The keeper replies, "I am supposed to be in the race tomorrow. That means I have to leave to spend the night on Man-O-War Cay. Because there is no one else to light the Elbow Reef Lighthouse, I cannot go."

UP thinks to himself, *surely it is not too difficult, even for a little lizard like me. I will volunteer to do it.*

"I know I can do this," he insists to the keeper. "I have watched you many times and I have friends that I can call if I need help."

"Are you sure I can count on you?" questions the lighthouse keeper.

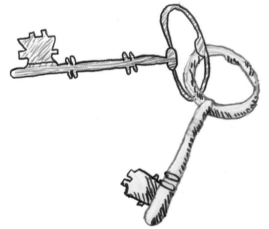

UP replies with utmost confidence, "DoN't Worry, I've got tHiS."

The lighthouse keeper gives him the keys. "I'm trusting you, UP."

The keeper smiles and jumps into a boat to go sailing. As he drifts behind a big yacht, he yells, "If you need more help, just. . . !"

UP cannot hear the rest. He shrugs, then jogs home, not caring much about what the keeper had to say.

When UP arrives at the Lizard Lodge, he finds his mother cooking his favourite dinner, ant casserole.

UP explains the keeper's situation to her and asks for permission to stand-in as the keeper for the night. She thinks about it for a minute, then says, "UP, do you know that the lighthouse is 89 feet high and there are 101 steps to the lantern room?

"So can I go?" UP begs, "Oh please, please?"

"Well . . . Okay," she agrees.

"I'm trusting you, UP. But be careful and pay attention to what you are doing. If you were to fall from the top. . . ." She stops, then continues, "I am just a little worried. Don't break anything, don't run up the stairs, don't hang over the railing. . . Wait . . . do you know how to . . ."

But UP is not listening. He is already out the door.

UP is super excited. He runs to ask his friend Abby, the Abaco Parrot, if she wants to have the coolest sleepover ever at the Elbow Reef Lighthouse.

"It will not be too dark, right? I hate the dark!" Abby squawks.

"Don't worry," UP assures her. "The lights will be on and we will have flashlights."

Then UP and Abby call their friend Joe.

Joe works on the Froggies boat, so he knows a lot about diving. Joe is an enormous orange frog who loves the colour green. "I'll meet you there and you should probably bring food, drinks and our favourite games, Gecko Stick and Lizard Lolly," proposes Abby.

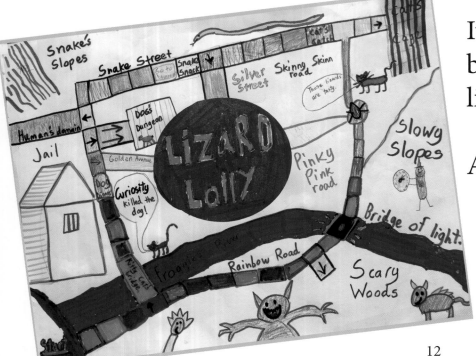

It is no surprise that they both say **YES!** to UP's lighthouse adventure.

And so the journey begins.

Joe and UP stop by a seagrape tree where they collect a giant leaf and a few small branches. They use the branches as oars to help steer their seagrape leaf 'boat' across the harbour to the light-house dock.

While paddling, UP looks around the harbour and watches the turtles pop their heads in and out of the water.

Just then, a gigantic boat enters the harbour at high speed and creates a big wake. The waves knock their paddle boat over!

UP and Joe watch as it floats away. They are both good swimmers, but the dock looks pretty far away. Just as they are about to panic, they see a pod of dolphins. The friendly dolphins swim over to them. UP recognizes that one of them is his good friend Donald.

They climb on to the dolphins' backs and are carried over to the lighthouse dock.

"I guess they didn't see the sign that says 'Slow Down You're in Hope Town!' " Donald chuckles. UP and Joe laugh and agree, "It's good to have friends!"

They thank them and walk up to the lighthouse.

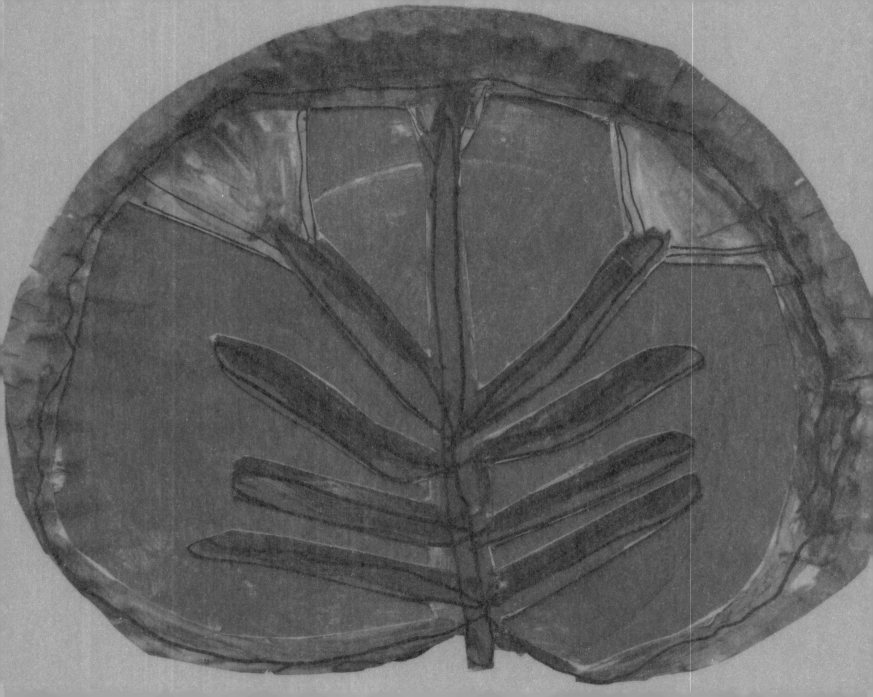

17

Then the keeper's dog, Ralph the potcake, starts chasing them.

The door to the keeper's quarters is locked. It will take too long to open it, so they run into the lighttower and close the door.

They wait and wait for the dog to go but he won't leave.

"It's time to light the lighthouse," UP announces. But just as he is about to light it, he stops.

"What happened?" wonders Abby who has just arrived through the open window.

"I… I… I've forgotten how to do it."

"Oh no, not good," mutter the friends. "What do we do?"

"I heard the keeper say something, but I didn't hear the end," replies UP.

"Why don't we just ask his dog?" suggests Abby.

"What? Are you nuts? He will eat me up!" exclaims UP.

Finally, they decide to ask the dog to help them. Joe has some unopened crackers in his pocket, and in exchange for the crackers, the dog agrees not to eat UP or his friends.

No one wants to see the light not lit, not even the dog!

As the sun is setting, they watch through the windows to see the sky turn purple, pink and orange.

"I remember that the first step is to check the pressure in the kerosene tanks. There is the hand pump right there," directs Joe.

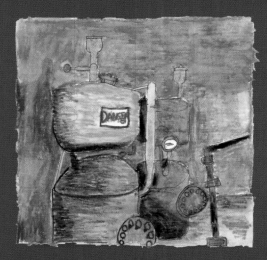

They try and try, but they are not strong enough to pump it. Luckily, their new friend Ralph helps out. After checking that the pressure is good, the friends suddenly notice it is becoming very dark outside.

Ralph gets the matches and they head up to the lantern room together.

"I can fly you to the top," announces Abby.

"I am glad my mom just taught me how to light a match," boasts UP as he climbs the ladder into the Fresnel lens. But before UP is able to strike the match, a commotion of flapping black wings stops him. It looks like a bat!

"WHo are you?" Abby gasps.

"I'm Berry the Bat and I live up here. I was just hanging in the petroleum burner and I thought you were going to barbeque me!" screeches Berry.

Berry asks, "Aren't you going to take the curtains down? You're supposed to do that first. The curtains protect the lantern room from the powerful daytime sun, but at night the lantern's light can't go through them," he explains.

Willie Berry and Abby remove the curtains that cover the lens, UP preheats the burner and places the match by the mantle, igniting it to make a burning flame.

Golden beams shine over the horizon. "It's working!" they all shout at once.

What an amazing sight. What an honour to be here. But now that it's lit, how are they ever going to stay up all night?

Suddenly, they get an idea. Leaving Ralph on duty, they venture into town. This time, they fly across the harbour on Abby's back.

After they treat themselves to a coffee at the Coffee House, they turn to admire the lighthouse's unique flash pattern—a series of five white flashes every 15 seconds.
But, something is wrong.
It is not flashing . . . in fact,
the lens is not even turning!

"YiKeS!" squawks Abby.
"OH No!" croaks Joe.
"OopS" utters UP.

They wonder what the problem is. It is only then, UP remembers he was supposed to wind the mechanism first, after that, the lens clock has to be wound every two hours!

On the way back across they fly over their friend Sirena, the beautiful mermaid. "Hi guys! What are you doing?" she asks.

"Tonight I am the lighthouse keeper," UP brags with pride.

"Wow, that sounds exciting! Can I help?" she squeals.

UP isn't sure that he needs any more help, but he does not want to disappoint his friend. He thinks for a second and suggests, "Sure! If you see the light not flashing again, climb on up and I will see what we can find for you to do."

UP, Abby and Joe wind the lens mechanism to get it turning. 1, 2, 3 . . . 101, 102, 103 . . . 200 . . . 300 . . . 400 . . . 426! After 426 full cranks, now it's working!

Then they go to the lantern room and set their alarm for the next winding.

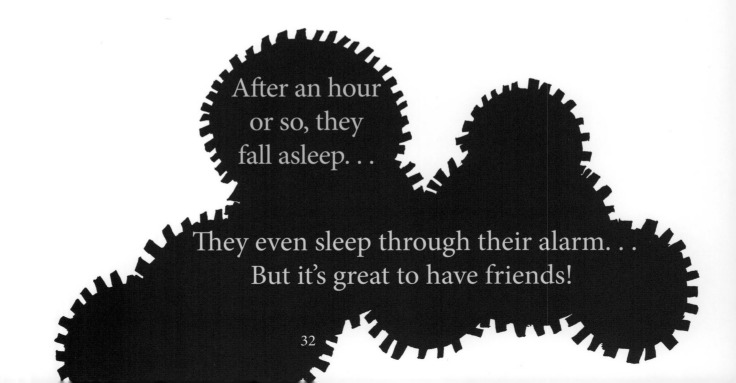

After an hour or so, they fall asleep. . .

They even sleep through their alarm. . . But it's great to have friends!

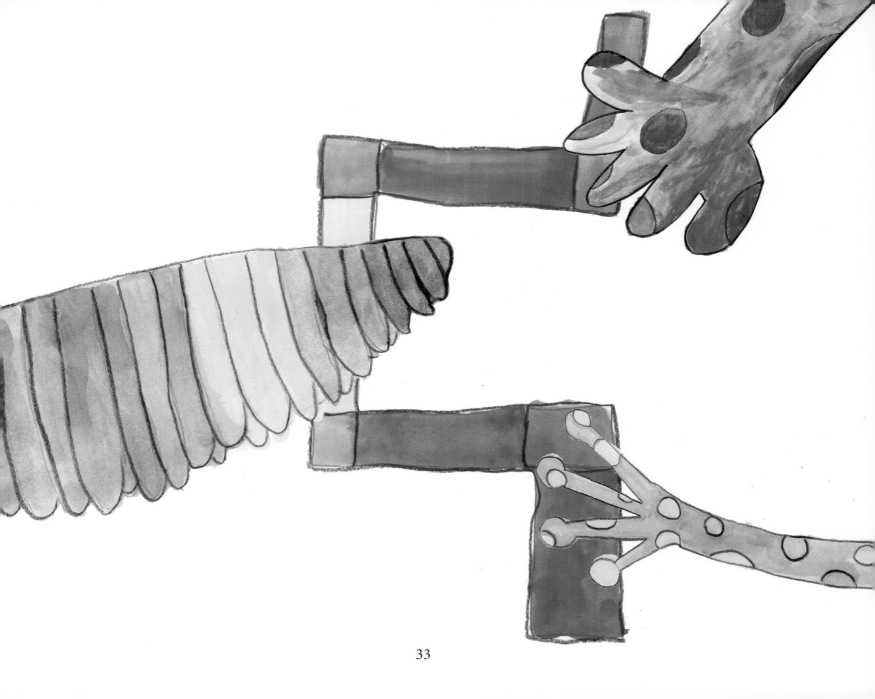

33

Berry, who is nocturnal, is hanging in a nearby tree, wide awake and bored.

He flies up to the lantern room and finds UP, Abby, Joe and Ralph fast asleep.

"WaKe Up!" screams Berry. "Aren't you supposed to wind the lens mechanism again?"

"You're right, I have to wind the machinery every two hours. What am I going to do?" asks UP.

"We should stay awake by playing games," recommends Abby. After a few games, Berry returns to his tree, never expecting that they would all soon fall asleep again.

This time, it is Sirena who notices the light is not flashing. She swims up to the dock at the lighthouse and sings a song to alert her friends. When they do not wake, she wraps her arms around the lighthouse and climbs it like a coconut tree. She pops her head through the little door at the top and finds the friends in dreamland and is unable to wake them.

She yells down to Donald the dolphin. "Looks like they are in a deep sleep. What do we do?"

"I have an idea," Donald says. "Here is some water. Wake them up." Then he sprays a fountain of water as high as the lighthouse out of his blow hole. Sirena reaches out her tail and splashes the water against the glass to wake them.

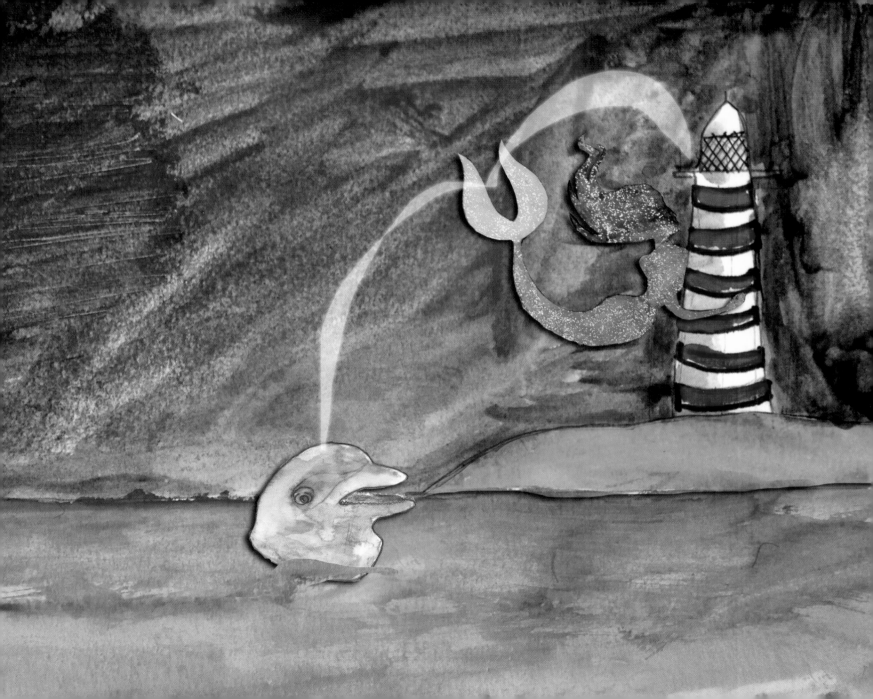

UP wakes up so surprised. "I can't believe I fell asleep again!"

"We will not let you fail," assures the mermaid. "It's good to have friends. I will send over my pal, Sideways, the land crab, to watch over you. If he sees you falling asleep again, he can pinch you to wake you up."

Pretty soon, Sideways sees their eyes closing and gives them a pinch and shouts, "ROUNd tHe troopS! PicK Up tHe pace!"

This is just the encouragement that UP and his friends need to stay awake.

Forward

Upward

Onward

Together

39

"OK, let's keep this thing cranking," exclaims UP. "We have to make sure the light shines and flashes all night!"

As they admire the signature pattern of flashes, they notice a ship in the distance.

"JUSt iN tiMe!" yells UP. "We've done it! The sailors can see us and now they know where the reef is."

They all happily shout, "We SaVed a SHip by KeepiNg tHe LigHt ON!"

"That was a close call," UP admits as he finally realizes how important it is to pay attention.

The next morning, the lighthouse keeper returns. He can see that UP has understood just how big a responsibility the lighthouse keeper's job is. The keeper hugs UP and jokes with him, "I can tell you have learned that many hands make 'light' work! Thank you UP." Then, he tells them all about the regatta and how he won the first place trophy.

UP beams with pride, knowing he and his friends have also won their own race. By working together as a team, they have learned to keep ships safe and the light on and shining brightly.

THE END

by Meredith Knowles.

Approximately 80 hours of art class time in various mediums collectively illustrate the story.

Artists and Authors:

Grade 6: Johnny Decius, Jason François, Fiona Guinness, Aaliyah Jean-Noel, Rashawn Joseph, Ryan Knowles and Megan McCully.

Grade 5: Jasmin Aberle, Harmony Bain, Ryelle Cornish, Katlyn Lederhause, Janeahy Loran, Maitland Lowe, Grant Malone, Eljdini Philogene, Erik Poëll, Lauren Sandberg, Lisa Saintil and Colby Stebbins.

Grade 4: Trey Evans, Journey Higgs, Cameron Jean, Renelda Jean, Maison Koepke, Casey Lightbourn, Ethan Lowe, Devon Malone, Luke Prosa, Ryleigh Sweeting and Dawson Thompson.

Grade 3: Kayla Albury, Jack Guinness, Monica Joseph, Meredith Knowles, Frye McCoy, Ian McCully, Whithiery Mildor, Alexandria Lederhause and Ella Russell.

Cover:	Sideways the crab by Ryelle Cornish. Joe by Lisa Saintil. Sailboat/water by Erik Poëll. Lightstation by Luke Prosa. Keeper by Fiona Guinness. UP by Katlyn Lederhause. Ralph by Rashawn Joseph. Berry the bat by Johnny Decius. Seagrape leaf by Whithiery Mildor. Abby by Ryleigh Sweeting.
Page 1:	Lighthouse painting by Meagan McCully.
Page 3:	Lizard lodge by Whithiery Mildor. Balcony by Alexandria Lederhause. UP by Katlyn Lederhause.
Page 4:	Dinghy dock by Fiona Guinness. Keeper by Fiona Guinness. UP by Ryan Knowles.
Page 5:	Sailboats by Luke Prosa.
Page 6:	Upper Key by Devon Malone. Lower Key by Cameron Jean.
Page 7:	Sailboat/water/houses by Journey Higgs. Keeper by Fiona Guinness.
Page 8:	UP, ants and doorway by Renelda Jean.
Page 9:	UP's mother by Ryan Knowles. Kitchen by Katlyn Lederhause. Dining Room by Grant Malone. Mermaid wall poster by Ella Russell.
Page 10:	Plants/sky by Dawson Thompson. UP by Journey Higgs.
Page 11:	Abby/plants/sky by Renelda Jean.
Page 12:	Lizard Lolly game, mask and snorkle by Colby Stebbins. Game dice by Ryan Knowles.
Page 13:	Froggies Building by Ryleigh Sweeting. Scuba tanks by Journey Higgs. Joe by Katlyn Lederhause.
Page 14:	Sky/Land/houses by Renelda Jean. Joe by Lisa Saintil. Seagrape leaf by Jack Guinness. UP by Ryan Knowles. Lower turtle by Maitland Lowe. Upper turtle by Lauren Sandberg. UP's oar by Ella Russell. Joe's oar by Kyla Albury.
Page 15:	Speedboat by Erik Poëll. Water by Colby Stebbins. Seagrape leaf by Meredith Knowles. Turtle by Janeahy Loran.
Page 16:	Dolphin by Katlyn Lederhause.
Overlay:	Seagrape leaf by Kyla Albury.
Page 17:	Donald the dolphin (left) by Erik Poëll. UP by Renelda Jean. Harbour/land by Journey Higgs. Frog by Harmony Bain. Top dolphin by Eljdini Philogene. Middle dolphin by Maitland Lowe. Slow down sign by Lauren Sandberg.

by Grant Malone and Luke Prosa

by Jack Guinness

Did you KNOW?

There are nearly 15,000 lighthouses spread around the globe. However, the lighthouse at the Elbow Reef Lightstation is the only remaining lighthouse in the world to be hand-cranked and kerosene burning.

Although the Elbow Reef Lightstation's grounds include the lighttower, keepers' quarters, store room, kitchen building and oil house, it seems the lighttower itself captures our attention the most. It consists of a concrete over brick tower topped with a two story metal (iron/bronze and copper) section called the "lantern."

Why were the Lighthouses in the Bahamas built?

The Imperial Lighthouse Service (ILS) commissioned their building and Trinity House in London hired the designers. The lightstations were built between 1836-1887 when The Bahamas was still a colony of Great Britain.

With the increase in shipping after the American Revolution and the amount of cargo now going back and forth between Great Britain, Europe and the Americas, there were more sailing ships transiting the hazardous shallow banks and current-filled channels of The Bahamas. Ships were constantly stranding and men and cargoes were lost. The British government built the Bahamian lightstations to guide sailing ships safely through the deep water channels between the island groups within the Bahamian Archipelago.

How many Bahamian ILS Lightstations are there?

There are eleven ILS lightstations in The Bahamas but only Elbow Reef Lightstation remains active, non-electrified and hand-wound. Of the unmanned automated lights, few are currently working. Aside from Elbow Reef Lightstation, only San Salvador (Dixon Hill) and Great Inagua (Mathewtown) Lights have lightkeepers.

The other lightstations in The Bahamas are at Hole in the Wall (Abaco); Gun Cay; Cay Sal; Great Isaac; Cay Lobos; Great Stirrup; Castle Island (Acklins); Bird Rock (Crooked Island); Great Inagua; San Salvador. The Lighthouse at Paradise (Hog) Island was built by the British in 1817 but it predates the ILS lights.

What is a lightstation?

A lighthouse refers to a single building housing the lighting apparatus. A lightstation is a self contained cluster of structures manned by keepers whose job is to keep the light on.

How tall is the lighttower?

The lighttower is 89 feet tall.

How high does the light shine?

The beam shines out 120ft. above mean high water (average height of sea level at high tide). 120ft. equals the height of the tower plus the height of the hill on which the lighttower sits.

How far out to sea can the light's beam be seen?

The light can be seen 15-20 miles out to sea.

How many steps are there to the watch room?

There are 101 steps between the entry (ground floor) and the watch room, the floor in which the lens rotating machinery sits.

What is the arrow on the top of the lighthouse for?

The arrow on the top of the lighthouse is a wind vane which points to the direction from which the wind is blowing. The vane is sheathed in copper and turns on small ballbearings. This vaned system is very common among British colonial lighthouses around the world, but is rarely, if-ever, seen on lighthouses in the United States.

How many lightkeepers are there?

There are now two permanent keepers at the lightstation. Presently they are Elvis Parker and Jeffery Forbes, Jr. In the past, the standard system during the ILS days was to employ three keepers—a principal keeper, an assistant keeper and an occasional keeper for times when one of the other keepers needed vacation or sick leave.

What is the source of the lighthouse's beam?

The bright beam of the light is fueled by vapourized kerosene ignited within the Hood Petroleum Vapour Burner (1910) which sits within the big Fresnel lens. The burner has a mantle which remains lit as long as there is vapourized fuel passing through it.

The burner itself is stationary. It is the rotation of the lens that causes the shafts of light to look as though they are moving, passing through the night sky.

What is a mantle?

A mantle is a small bag-shaped mesh cloth that sits on the top of the burner. It is what glows brightly when the burner is lit and the vapourized fuel passes through it. A mantle is distinguished from a wick in that it is hollow. The mantles are made of rayon and a tiny amount of a rare earth element which remains once the rayon in the mantle has burned off.

Our current mantles which are custom made in Wichita, Kansas, by the Coleman Company, usually last 2-4 weeks. Once burned off, they are fragile, very brittle and can easily be damaged.

Why use kerosene for the fuel?

When the lighthouse was built in 1864, other fuels were used including whale oil and vegetable oils. But once it became available in the 1870s, kerosene (called paraffin or petroleum by the British) became the most cost-effective fuel. Because no steady source of electricity was available in the The Bahamas in the1930s, the Hood PV burners were installed.

What is the vapourizer?

The vapourizer is the metal part of the burner within which the heated fuel changes from liquid to gas.

How long does it take to preheat the vapourizer?

It takes 5-10 minutes in summer and 10-15 minutes in the winter.

Tell me more about the lens.

The lighthouse at Elbow Reef Lightstation has a 5 bulls-eye first-order Fresnel lens. It was built in 1927 by the Chance Brothers in Birmingham, England. Its glass, bronze frame work and carriage weigh over 7000 pounds.

What causes the lens to turn?

The keepers! They must hand-crank the clockwork lens-turning machinery every two hours throughout the night. There is a handle on the geared system in the watch room that the keepers must turn. It takes 426 turns, or *crinkes* as Jeff calls them, to raise the weights the full amount.

Weights? What for?

The weights are on a wire cable and travel up and down inside the column in the middle of the light tower. The action of the weights lowering, transferred through a series of gears in the machinery, keeps the lens in motion. 700 lbs. of weights are housed in the hollow cavity of the central column within the lighttower.

The weights are made of iron and lead. Look at the door-stop at the entryway to the lighttower- it is actually a half-weight.

Why is the electric light used on some nights?

Sometimes the kerosene is not available or the fuel is dirty and has caused a flare-up of the burner so it is necessary for the keepers to use electricity. The 100+ year old burners can be temperamental.

Why not use electricity all the time?

The Elbow Reef Lightstation is the only hand-cranked kerosene burning lighthouse remaining in the world. What a shame it would be to lose the very last one. We want to keep the light on. Some days in Abaco, kerosene can be more reliable than electricity!

How can you help with restoration efforts?

Thank you for purchasing this book, a tangible collection of children's efforts to help the public visualize the historical and nautical importance of our lighthouse. Our restoration and preservation efforts are for future generations to enjoy. To learn how you may make a contribution, please feel free to contact Ms. Lory Kenyon, *Executive Director, Elbow Reef Lighthouse Society* at erlsbahamas@gmail.com or Heather Forde-Prosa, *Secretary, Elbow Reef Lighthouse Society* at Heatherprosa@gmail.com.

INSide tHe Art classes

by Jason François

Dedicated art teacher **Grade 6**: Attila Feszt.
The exceptional talents and learning potential of these students required specific attention. Not only did the kids have a lot of fun with him, but they had fun producing their art. This is evident in the host of characters created in chalk pastels including the character of the keeper who is an indigenous Bahamian rock iguana.

by Fiona Guinness

by Whithiery Mildor

Dedicated art teachers **Grade 3**: Deanne Albury and Aimee Lederhause introduced the kids to technique, color and creativity. Village art on pg. 43 was inspired by winter resident, Abbey Griffin.

by Jack Guinness

by Maitland Lowe   by Trey Evans

From sailboats to landscapes to light-houses, Bill County taught us his tricks and helped us with our confidence in handling the watercolor medium.

by Aaliyah Jean-Noel

Dual purpose: Some of our art pieces were designed to fit into the themes of national art contests, but others were produced to fulfill a fundraising opportunity. The Grade 4's created 16" x 16" collages that mixed latex, tempera, and glitter paints with origami paper. These artworks were all sold and the funds raised were used to buy a new stove for the lighthouse keepers.

by Cameron Jean

by Janeahy Loran

The mosaic style sea turtles were inspired by our friend and local artist, Barefoot Contessa who paints island scenes on silk.

by Devon Malone

The flying Parrot was taught by nature artist, Susan Roberts, who specializes in wildlife and seascape paintings.

by Trey Evans

The key is a very important symbol in the book because:
1) it represents the shared responsibility UP and his friends in Hope Town feel for the lightstation. 2) its transfer from keeper to local community members is symbolic of the transfer of lighthouse oversight from Dave Gale to the Elbow Reef Lighthouse Society.
3) "Up Keep" is the 'key' to maintaining a lighthouse. Our children and grandchildren will also be handed this task.
The key class was assisted by student intern, Kora Wilhoyte.

UP Project creative director and dedicated art teacher **Grades 4 and 5**: Heather Forde-Prosa. She was often assisted in class by one or more of her artistic friends: Bill County, Susan Roberts, Susan Sandberg, Lisa Ballard, Mary Balzac, Teleri Jones or Stephanie Sweeting.

Dog: Lauren Sandberg
Frog: Katlyn Lederhause
Tanks: Ryleigh Sweeting

Up-cycled Works of Art:

We used recycled materials where possible because we are a green school.

by Harmony Bain

Lens project: Made with recycled packaging foil, water bottles, paper plates, plastic cup rims and lids. Black construction paper made the iron, and the chalk pastels drawn over the black paper created the reflections.

by Trey Evans

Four hours of class time but worth it! Astrobright neon paper collage with watercolor paint washes and recycled tin foil for the doors and windows. Classes were assisted by Mary Balzac.

by Frye McCoy

Seagrape leaves were made from paper plates. It took two plates to make one leaf. We started with a painted background on the base plate and a cut out detailed layer over the top.

by Jasmin Aberle

The reef became another use for puffed rice cereal. The cereal was glued to paper and painted in colourful coral and sealife colors.

by Eljdini Philogene

Amos Ferguson, the late Bahamian artist known for his primitive style paintings, inspired the crab artwork which we painted on cardboard canvases with latex house paint tinted with tempura paints. We also used his technique of marking the canvas with nail heads. Assisted by Lisa Ballard.

by Grant Malone and Luke Prosa

Cardboard has a great ochre color that complements colors drawn or painted directly on it. Local businesses receive excessive amounts of cardboard packing boxes that we are happy to reuse for projects.